D1532653

Beacon

the Bright Little Firefly

Written by Joe Troiano   Illustrated by Susan Banta

This book is dedicated to one of the great beacons in my life, my friend, Jack.   —J. T.

Backpack Books • Holiday Hill Farm

Copyright © 2002 by Holiday Hill Enterprises, LLC.
Holiday Hill Farm and Beacon, the Bright Little Firefly™ Copyright and Trademark Holiday Hill Enterprises, LLC.
All rights reserved. No part of this book may be used or reproduced in any manner whatsoever without the written permission of the Publisher.
2002 Backpack Books™ Published under exclusive license by Backpack Books™, a division and trademark of Michael Friedman Publishing Group, Inc.
ISBN 0-7607-3210-8   Printed and bound in Italy
10 9 8 7 6 5 4 3 2 1

Did you know that fireflies love the Fourth of July?
It's true.
They do.
Here's the reason why—
they believe all the fireworks they see in the sky
are really giant fireflies flying by.

It all began a long time ago
when a firefly named Beacon chose not to glow.

You see, fireflies had a rule they all had to obey—
every firefly had to glow exactly the same way.

First on . . .

then off . . .

then count to ten . . .

then on . . .

then off . . .

then start
    over again.

Each firefly going along with the crowd
because glowing your own way just wasn't allowed.

But Beacon marched to a different drum.
He thought flashing your taillight ought to be fun!
He believed every firefly should have the right
to decide when and where to light its light.

So one night in the meadow when it was time to glow
Beacon turned off his light and just said, "No!"
And when every other firefly shut his or her light
Beacon turned his on EXTRA bright.

It got so confusing that before very long
every firefly in the sky was flashing all wrong.

They started to argue,
then they started to fight
about who was lit wrong,
and who was lit right.

But they all knew who started the trouble that night,
so Beacon was grounded!
He had to shut off his light.

But he knew he was right.
He knew it through and through.
And after that Fourth of July
everyone else knew it too.

The Holiday Hill Farm fireworks display
takes place down in the meadow each Independence Day.

Families and friends gather around
and spread bedsheets and blankets all over the ground.

Then they "oooh" and they "aaah" at the rocket's red glare
and stare up at the colors that burst in the air.

But that night when rain clouds came rolling by
they had to stop all the fireworks on the Fourth of July!

Beacon the firefly was sitting nearby
when a pretty little girl began to cry.
He knew it was time to shine his light
and prove, once and for all, that he was right.

He flew through the crowd.
He flew high.
He flew low.

He flew onto that little girl's nose
and started to glow.

Then he flew to the next boy and girl down the row
and performed his own little fireworks show.

He started out flashing two DOTS and a DASH!

Then he flickered a little quicker
    DOT DOT DASH DOT DASH!

Soon every child, in every row,
was watching Beacon, the bright little firefly, put on a show.

The other fireflies realized that Beacon was right—
every firefly should be free to light his or her light
whenever they want,
no counting to ten,
no flashing the same way again and again.

Then one
    by one
        by one
            by one,
            they flew over to Beacon and joined in the fun.

And for the finale
Beacon knew just what to do.
He flew through the raspberries and the blueberries too,
then he flew back to the meadow, covered in goo,
and turned on his light . . . it was red, white, and blue!

The children all cheered as Beacon flew by
proudly flashing his taillight that Fourth of July.
And he was the happiest firefly you ever did see,
in the home of the brave, and the land of the free.

So the next time you see fireworks high in the sky,
imagine that they're Beacon and his friends flying by.

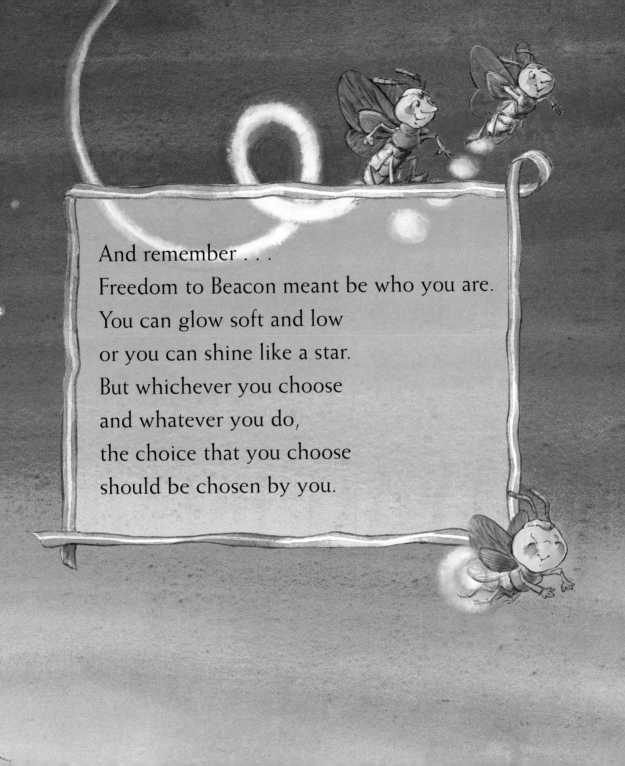

And remember . . .
Freedom to Beacon meant be who you are.
You can glow soft and low
or you can shine like a star.
But whichever you choose
and whatever you do,
the choice that you choose
should be chosen by you.

And if you forget
don't get upset!

Look out your window on a hot summer night
and watch how differently each firefly lights its light.